Muscovy Ma

Minding Your Manners

To Katie
with best wishes
from Helen and
the ducks

Helen Kendall Smith

Published by Helen Kendall Smith
www.muscovymansion.com

Comments and observations are the opinion of the author only.

ISBN 978-0-9572486-1-8

Printed by Information Press
Designed by Touchmedia

Acknowledgements

A loyal faithful bird, the Muscovy given time love and patience
will come to call and become a lifetime friend.
Dedicated to Muscovy all over the world, often very much misunderstood.

Thank you to:
My parents for their patience and especially to my father for sharing his photographic expertise.
Geoff for his patience and backbreaking worm digging.
My friends and family for putting up with my Muscovy obsession.
Dr Maureen Sears.
Graham Hicks.
Jo Rothery.
Aston Pottery, Aston, Oxfordshire.
All who assisted in the creation and continuation of Muscovy Mansion.

The sun is shining,
the skies are blue,
Mother is calling out to you.

"Get up, wake up,
come on – up you get.
Wash that face and
make sure you get it wet.

"Clean your teeth and in your haste
don't forget to use toothpaste."

"No we will not, we want to sleep," they said.
Under the covers stayed the sleepyheads.

"I beg your pardon?"
we all heard Mother cry.
"Teenagers," she whispered
with a sigh.

"Come on, come on –
now don't be a pest.
I don't want to have to leave this nest!

"I don't understand it,
when I was young,
we were up, out,
looking for some fun.

"None of this lazing around all day,
bedroom floor covered with socks.

"And certainly no Television, iPads, Playstation or Xbox!

"I do not agree with 'things of today'
Outdoors unless it is raining –
if I had my way!

"Walking the plank,
crossing the river.
Falling in, it made you shiver!

Playing in puddles,
jumping in waterfalls,
meeting your friends –
used to be 'fun' for all.

"Time for school,
you are going to be late.

"Your sister is ready and waiting by the gate."

"What would you like in your snack box dear?
Come on, come on," she said.

"I thought I made it quite clear,
there is no time for lounging in bed!"

"An apple? A sandwich –
perhaps you would like cheese?"

"An apple," came the shout.
But without a please –
yes, without a please.

"I think there is no occasion
nor any excuse

for not minding ones
Ps and Qs.

"I hope you remember
your manners at school
and do as you are told
and stick to the rules."

"Of course I do" he said,
trying a different tack –

but he crossed his fingers
behind his back.

Uncle Cloud looked at him...

and his friend Ernie looked at him...

and he thought they knew...

He looked down quickly,
for not a word he said was true!

"What would you like for breakfast?
Cereal or toast?

"I have that chocolate spread you like the most.

"And perhaps some juice
to go with it?"

"No, I am looking for my sports kit."

"Remember your inhaler,
in case you start to wheeze.

"This cold, frosty weather can make you sneeze!"

"Of course, of course,
I am off now, bye bye.
"See you later,"
she heard his brother cry.

And so Mother waved them off
as they ran.
She cleared up from breakfast
and her chores began.

Mother started to clean the sink and

with her sister helping,
she started to think

of how she could remind her
brood to watch their Ps and Qs.

Manners are very important –
the ducklings must learn this, too.

The ladies talked
and Mother thought
until time for their return,

by which time she had a plan
of rewards they could earn.

Simple ways to encourage
with a please and thank you,
for manners are essential.

The 'modern' way just will not do.

Upon their return they were greeted warmly with fun.

Mother really does love
all her little ones.

Sky wanted to play on Xbox,
Playstation or TV.

Mother told no-one
to play with him
until after homework and his tea.

Sky said crossly,
"Where is friend Ernie?
I thought I saw him inside."

Ernie was there,
but he was trying to hide!

“Uncle Cloud, I am looking for Grandpa, I want to play.”

"Well he might be cooling his feet after a hard working day.

"I do know where he is, but –
reflect on it, is all I can say!"

The iPad had gone, the Playstation,
TV and Xbox locked away.
The key in her hand would stay there
until she heard them say...

"Please Mother" and "thank you"
afterwards, too.
Manners soon became
everyone's point of view.

"Thank you Mother,
for waking me up,"
he said, not in his usual way.
"Is it today Jedward is coming
to play?

"I shall come down right now,"
and he got dressed straight away.

"Please may I have apple juice?"
he asked

and Mother her smile
she could barely mask.

The simple ways to teach children are not unkind,

but manners open many doors,
you will find.

Muscovy Mansion

Muscovy Mansion has been created by the author specifically to encourage a love of reading and the Muscovy breed itself. The adventures of the real Muscovy on a day-to-day basis are here to captivate parents and children alike. Enjoy reading about the adventures of these real, living Muscovy characters, owned and photographed on a daily basis by the author, for whom they are much-loved pets.

A word about Muscovy

Muscovy, the only duck the author breeds, is actually a South American Goose. The Latin name for Muscovy is 'Cairina Moschata'. Muscovy are allowed to run wild in many countries. Characters in each book are played by real Muscovy who live at home or belong to friends. Muscovy have a preening gland which necessitates their access to fresh water to bathe and waterproof daily, also to drink. The gestation period for a Muscovy is 35 days from the start of incubation. Muscovy ducklings can take up to and sometimes more than 48 hours to escape from their shells using their specially formed 'egg tooth' used for breaking the egg. This tooth is discarded later as there is no longer a use for it.

Muscovy ducks are beautiful ducklings that develop into large birds with claws on their webbed feet for roosting in the trees. More pronounced in the males, 'caruncles' or red lumps on their faces grow during adolescence to adulthood. While a Muscovy duckling is adorably beautiful, many find the grown duck not so handsome. Muscovy ducks live for a long time and are prolific breeders, laying eggs on a daily basis into their dotage. Muscovy need to free range on grass and as a result, lay creamy, oval eggs. The unique bobbing greeting and gentle low voice of the Muscovy ensure their continued popularity.

Created in and around the Cotswolds

Kelmscott Manor

The Swan Hotel, Radcot

St Mary's Church, Fairford

Also in the series

Muscovy Mansion
Not a Real Turtle

A very large parcel has arrived at Muscovy Mansion. The ducks have no idea what is in it and when the content is revealed, the ducks have no idea what it is for.